Dear Reader

Recently, I read a fascinating newspaper article about the discovery of some ancient figs in a Stone Age village in Jordan. I started thinking about the people who had lived there, 10 000 years ago – and then I wondered if there were heroes and villains in those days, too. Just like a fig tree, the idea for this story started to grow and grow!

John Parsons
Author

The Jordanian Mountains

1. Gilgal
2. The site of present-day Dan'har
3. Ibn Kayid's cave

1 Prologue

When the clapping and cheering from the audience died down, Melissa Fox moved to the microphone and took a deep breath.

She looked at the crowd of delegates to the International Convention on Archaeology that she was about to address. As the applause demonstrated, Melissa was well known to the delegates, all experts in the field of archaeology. Her specialty, re-creating the stories of ancient civilisations through the remains they left behind, always enthralled her colleagues.

But this time, she was about to embark upon a different story. Tonight, Melissa's story would be far from the world of dry bones, fragments of tools and the rubble of ancient buildings that enthused archaeologists the world over.

Tonight's story was a tale of drama and deception. The story of a crime, hidden for ten thousand years. The story of a mystery that had lain forgotten across ten millennia.

"Thank you, friends and colleagues," began Melissa Fox. She gazed once more at the expectant faces, four hundred people, all focusing on her. Then, after a second's hesitation, she began.

2 The Pistachio Grove

"In 2006, archaeologists on the west bank of the Jordan River were working on a site from the late Stone Age, or Neolithic era, as we call it. At the time, I read the results of their research with interest – but little did I know that the things they uncovered would help me solve an ancient crime.

As in all good mysteries, I won't give away the clues right at the start. But I will say that the work of these archaeologists inspired me to start my current research in that region.

My story begins in October 2010. Those of you who have worked in Jordan will know that, while the sun is warm and skies are clear in spring and autumn, winter is cold and rainy. Snowfall in the highlands is common in December, and often the trails throughout the mountainous areas are closed after heavy rainfall.

That autumn, on one of my rare days off, I'd been hiking along one of the trails in the mountains, when I spied an area that sparked my interest. My work at the site I'd originally come to Jordan for was nearing completion. Most of the artefacts there had been documented, researched and moved to the Jordan Archaeological Museum in Amman, the capital of Jordan.

I was keen to find a new project. And that afternoon, as I rested on the plateau in a grove of wild pistachios, which the locals call *fustuq halabee*, something caught my eye.

The last season's rain had caused a minor mudslide, now reduced to a scattering of dry rocks and rubble. Among the debris, my eyes fell upon a handful of rocks that seemed too even in their dimensions to be natural.

All of you, ladies and gentlemen, will have experienced that moment when wonder turns to certainty and the thrill of discovery raises the hairs on the back of your neck.

After scrambling down the incline and examining the rocks, I knew that they had been fashioned not by the wind and the rain, but by human hands. That afternoon in October 2010 was the moment when, once again, I felt that thrill of discovery.

Three hours later, with my back aching because of the unexpected rocks I now carried in my rucksack, I reached Dan'har, the village where I was staying for a few days. By the time dusk approached, the streets were filled with people. The aromatic smell of *mensaf*, the Jordanian dish of lamb and yoghurt, wafted from the lively cafes and restaurants. But I spent that evening alone in my room, poring over the rocks I had retrieved from my pistachio grove, high in the hills.

The next morning I rose early, ate some thyme-scented *manousheh* flatbread, and then went through the contacts list in my mobile phone. It didn't take me long to talk to the right authorities in Amman. My archaeological colleagues needed little persuading and, within a couple of hours, an expedition to uncover the secrets of the *fustuq halabee* grove was taking shape.

By the time the sun had reached its highest point at noon, my thoughts were filled with the excitement of a new project and a new story to be uncovered. But it was to be many days before the excitement of the real story behind the ancient events at the grove was to reveal itself."

3 A Stranger in the Valley

Ibn Kayid, whose name meant "the son of the cunning one", stood before the woven oak gates to Gilgal.

It had been seven days since Ibn Kayid had started his hurried escape along the river valley, picking his way along the rocky banks as fast as he could, trying to cover his tracks and outpace the members of the tribe that were pursuing him.

That year, the winter had been harsh. There were meagre stores of nuts, grains and wild fruits. Those stores meant the difference between life and death for the small family groups who foraged around the area in which Ibn Kayid had found himself. The temptation to raid the stores had proved too much for Ibn Kayid, who had been wandering the valley hungry and alone. Now, he was intent on escaping the wrath of the tribespeople and returning to the hidden cave that his father, Kayid, had built as a refuge high in the hills, many days walk to the north-east.

Eventually, after seven hungry days and seven cold nights, he reached Gilgal. He stood before the gates and called loudly.

"I am a stranger from the north-east. I mean no harm to you or your families."

From one of the stone huts clustered behind the gates, an old woman appeared and eyed Ibn Kayid suspiciously.

"What brings you here, stranger?" called the old woman.

"I seek shelter for the night," replied Ibn Kayid, nodding towards the fire burning in the midst of the huts. "I bring dried figs in return for a place to lay my head."

A moment later, a younger woman appeared behind the old woman.

"We have no need for figs," she said. "Be on your way."

Undeterred, Ibn Kayid reached into the goatskin pouch he carried slung over his shoulder. He drew out a handful of stolen pistachio nuts and let them trickle through his fingers back into the pouch.

"I have fustuq halabee *you may share," he enticed.*

As the pistachios clattered back into the pouch, the women exchanged glances. The younger woman called out.

"Fahd!"

Through the smoke, a young man appeared from one of the other stone huts. His skin was dark from days spent in the harsh sunlight, and he was swathed in skins and a blanket of knotted sheep's wool. As the young man emerged, Ibn Kayid noticed he was also carrying a heavy, gnarled stick with a fearsome stone axe head attached.

With the winter approaching, a stranger in the valley could be killed for much less than a pouch of fustuq halabee. *Ibn Kayid hesitated. Should he run or stay?*

The young man stared at Ibn Kayid and, to his relief, rested the axe beside the entrance to his hut.

"You may come within the walls of Gilgal," he said, keeping his hand within reach of the axe. "Sleep by the embers of our fire this night."

Ibn Kayid held his hands out, palms upward, to show his thanks. Then he walked through the gate of woven oak saplings.

"By what name are you known?" asked the young man.

Ibn Kayid thought quickly. To be known as the son of the cunning one did not put others at ease.

"I am known as Ghayyath," he lied. "The one who helps."

"I am known as Fahd," said the man. Ibn Kayid nodded. The cheetah. If Fahd was as swift and powerful as the feared predator of the lowlands, he would have to be careful around this man.

"This is my sister, Durriyyah, named for the glittering stars," continued the young man, nodding at the younger woman. "And our father's sister, Shamar."

Knowledge, nodded Ibn Kayid, his curiosity immediately aroused. What did this older woman know?

A handful of other faces, all female, peered out at the new arrival from the darkness of their huts.

"Where are the other men?" asked Ibn Kayid.

"They have been hunting to the west for these three days past," replied Fahd. As if to anticipate Ibn Kayid's next question, he raised the leather skin covering his left leg. Ibn Kayid gasped when he saw the crooked bone and terrible scar that rose from his thigh.

"I do not hunt," he said. "This makes me too slow."

Ibn Kayid nodded and, inside, he relaxed. He realised why this man bore the name of the cheetah. He had been lucky to survive the attack, which must have happened many summers before.

"Rest by our fire," said Fahd. "I will bring some water."

The young man headed back to his hut to fetch some water. Ibn Kayid, conscious of the stares of Durriyyah, Shamar and the other women, looked around the small village. And while the onlookers saw an innocent smile, they could not read the thoughts of Ibn Kayid, who was wondering what things the huts concealed that he might carry off before the next morning's dawn.

4 Back at the Grove

"By the time the end of October was approaching, I had secured permission from the authorities to conduct an exploratory examination of the site.

In the preceding days, my team and I had gathered in Dan'har. All were eager to start, so when notification arrived, everyone was excited.

The very next morning, we headed into the hills early – so early that we were half an hour along the track when we heard the first calls to prayer from Dan'har's minaret in the distance.

We pushed on and reached our destination within a couple of hours. I looked around the plateau and, at that moment, I was filled with anticipation. Beneath the roots of the pistachio trees and on the exposed slopes of the rocky scree, I was sure we would find a story that would add a new chapter to the book of knowledge about human civilisation.

Little did we know that we would not wait long for our story to present itself. Within a few days, we would uncover the elements we needed to tell our tale of those ancient days. But, like all archaeological sites, the elements, the 'words' to the story, would be all jumbled up. It was up to us to find the right order. Only then would the true story be revealed.

Our first task was to peg out the area so that we could examine each section of the site in an orderly fashion.

Once our pegs and our string lines had divided the site into manageable squares, we drew detailed maps of the area. This meant we could place any artefacts we found into an overall map, which might give extra meaning to our discoveries.

Next, we took detailed photographs of the area. Once we started work, the landscape would gradually be altered by holes and piles of discarded rubble. It was important to record the initial state of the site.

Finally, we examined the entire area in order to decide where we should start. The logical place was the rocky incline where I'd located the square blocks of rock. But we checked everywhere just to be sure I hadn't missed a better place to start.

After an hour, we gathered and all agreed that the rocky incline was indeed our most promising starting point.

Within another hour, we had all our equipment ready and the initial phase of our archaeological dig was about to start.

It was midday and I was keen to get going. I was about to ease my trowel into the dry soil around the rocks when someone called out.

'Wait!' they said. 'Let's have a photograph of Melissa Fox, about to start the exploration at the grove of the *fustuq halabee*.'

I smiled and played for the cameras for a few seconds. Then I started work.

Barely ten minutes had passed when I made the first discovery. I'd been working on a cluster of rocks that looked like they, too, had been hewn by hand. Then, as I loosened some soil, a cascade of the stones worked themselves free and tumbled about a metre down the slope, like a handful of dice that had been rolled by some ancient hand.

The others in the team gathered the rocks, one by one, and carefully numbered them with chalk. Then we climbed back up to the plateau. For the next few minutes, we examined the strangely square stones, convinced that they were not naturally shaped. Then, after some discussion, someone noticed something interesting.

'Most of the stones have the remains of a black dusty film on one of their faces,' they said. 'Could it be from an ancient fire?'

I looked at one of the stones. Perhaps this was the tell-tale sign of an old cooking fire? Were these simply the remains of a long-ago camp fire, assembled within a circle of stones that someone had arranged on the track?

At that moment, I was a little disappointed. I had hoped we would find evidence of a larger stone structure, a shelter built during the late Neolithic period. Campfires were usually temporary and revealed little of the people who had warmed themselves there. But I pressed on, determined to find evidence of a more permanent habitation. I was not to be disappointed.

Around one o'clock, with the sun high above the plateau, the heat was starting to slow us down, so we broke for some lunch in the shade of the pistachio trees. Then, after an hour's break, we started again with renewed energy. As I worked my way further and further through the square rocks in the incline, I suddenly struck something that I had not expected.

It was another square stone. Neatly wedged above it was another. And another.

As I scraped soil and debris away, more of the stones were revealed. A couple of minutes later, I took a step back. This was amazing. I had found an ancient stone wall."

5 A Forest of Figs

Ibn Kayid smiled at Shamar, who had brought an earthen bowl full of figs. Together with the other villagers, he warmed himself by the fire.

"Your figs are plentiful and good," he remarked, glancing around. "You are fortunate. Where I call home, the seeds of the fig will not grow."

"The seeds of this fig will not grow either," said Shamar. "And yet, there are many families that call Gilgal home. How do you suppose we manage to feed ourselves?"

"Hush," murmured Durriyyah, with a warning glance at her aunt.

But the old woman, who was not used to such an attentive audience, ignored her niece.

"I have a forest of figs in my hut," she boasted to Ibn Kayid.

Ibn Kayid did not understand. Fig trees sprang from the ground where, a year before, an old fruit had fallen.

And, most of the time, not even then. What could this old woman mean?

"A forest of figs?" said Ibn Kayid. He looked over at Shamar's hut. "Inside your hut?"

The old lady looked at Ibn Kayid triumphantly. "There are enough figs to feed everyone here for years to come," she declared. "All within a small wooden box that Fahd has fashioned for me."

"Shamar! Enough!" frowned Durriyyah. "Our visitor does not wish to hear your stories. Speak no more."

Reluctantly, the old woman fell silent, with a sullen look like that of a child denied their plaything. But the younger woman, Durriyyah, was wrong. Ibn Kayid did, indeed, wish to hear the stories of this magical fig forest within the old lady's hut. He resolved to find out more when the villagers had drifted off to sleep in their huts.

He faked a yawn and stretched his arms wearily.

"I shall sleep soon," he declared. "It has been many days walk from the fields where I gathered the fustuq halabee *I have shared with you tonight."*

"We will let you rest," said Durriyyah, motioning to her aunt and the remaining villagers. "We must sleep, too, for the men will return tomorrow and we will all be busy."

Ibn Kayid forced a smile, even though he did not welcome the news that the menfolk were soon to return. Still, it mattered not. All things going to plan, he would be well on his way to the cave in the hills hours before the men returned. All that remained for his night's work was to discover what exactly he would carry there.

He drew his skins around his shoulders and settled down by the light of the dying fire. But he did not sleep. Instead, he listened carefully until the noises of the villagers slowly died down. Then, when there was nothing but the sound of distant crickets and the breeze of the dry wind in the nearby oak and cypress trees, he carefully got to his feet and silently headed for Shamar's hut.

"Shamar, I see no fig forest! You have been weaving stories to a poor traveller," murmured Ibn Kayid coyly. He winked at the old lady. He could see she was enjoying the attention of a stranger.

Shamar beckoned him over. From under a pile of skins and knotted blankets, she withdrew a long wooden box. She slid open the lid and proudly displayed its contents.

Ibn Kayid frowned. There was no more than a handful of twigs in the box. This was no treasure worth stealing.

"I see you do not understand," said the old woman gleefully. "And, as you are not from Gilgal, I cannot expect you to."

Ibn Kayid looked at the old woman. What did she mean?

"I have told you that the seeds of our figs do not grow. But, less than an hour's walk through the forest, we have an endless supply of figs that grow in number year by year. How?"

Ibn Kayid shrugged. "I do not know, Shamar."

The old woman pointed to the twigs. "This is our secret," she winked conspiratorially. "The seeds will not grow. But fresh twigs, carefully cut from the branches in springtime, will grow. Each year, the twigs from a single tree burst forth into a forest of new trees."

Ibn Kayid had never heard such a strange tale.

"No," he said. "Without a seed, there can be no tree."

"No," corrected Shamar. "Without knowledge, there can be no tree."

Melissa Fox eyed her audience. They were spellbound, waiting for the next series of events to be revealed. She took another deep breath and continued her story.

"The moment we discovered the ancient wall, we knew we were onto something big. Neolithic ruins are not common, of course, but there are several sites throughout Jordan and the surrounding countries where they are to be found. Usually, they are merely the outlines of where a stone building once stood, or a few scattered artefacts within a collapsed pile of rubble. Finding a wall largely intact is rare.

Although the team was working all around the plateau, the news spread like wildfire and within minutes, everyone had gathered to gape at the astounding discovery.

I had a sudden thought.

'To have found a wall is exciting,' I said, gazing at the faces of my team. 'But the best part is that, with every wall, there comes something else.'

'What?' asked someone.

'The part that lies behind the wall,' I replied. 'Let's spend what hours we have left today uncovering the extent of this wall. Then, at the crack of dawn tomorrow, we will discover what lies behind.'

There wasn't a moment's hesitation. The entire team collected their equipment and it wasn't until dusk fell that we stopped.

As night arrived, the clear skies became filled with glittering stars. At a high altitude, far from the nearest city or town, there was no haze from cooking fires or glow from street lights to lessen the light from the stars. But the conversation that night was not about the undiscovered worlds that lay above our heads. It was about the undiscovered world that lay beneath our feet.

There would have been few of the team who didn't wake while it was still dark the next morning. But, as trained archaeologists, we knew we had to wait until first light before we started. Missing some clue in the dark, no matter how small, would be unforgiveable – so we waited impatiently for the sun to rise.

Once the pistachio trees around the grove were dappled with the morning's first sunlight, we began work.

First, we took photographs of the entire wall we had uncovered. Then, once we had a permanent record of how the stones were arranged, we carefully numbered each one. Then the exciting work began.

Carefully, so as not to collapse the entire structure, I levered one of the stones loose.

It took a few minutes because I could see from the sagging lines of rock that the wall had shifted during the millennia between when it had been erected and now. Nevertheless, after some scraping and jiggling, the first of the wall's rocks was dislodged.

I slowly withdrew it from the position it had held for ten thousand years. Then I stared in amazement at what I saw.

Behind the rock, there was nothing. A deep, dark nothing that stretched far into the hillside. This was amazing. The wall hid a cave!

My first instinct was to push through the remaining stones to discover what lay in the cave. But, of course, I couldn't do that. Each stone had to be carefully removed. It was a painstaking process but, as the hours passed, we slowly made a hole large enough to squeeze through.

'Bring some torches,' I said to one of the team. They hurried away, returning with three torches.

It was eleven o'clock. We had been working all morning for this moment. Now it was time to step through the hole in the wall, back into a place where I knew a human hadn't set foot in ten millennia.

Two of my assistants prepared to come inside the cave with me. We squeezed through the hole, eager to discover what lay inside the cave.

At first, the contrast between the bright sunlight outside and the inky darkness of the cave was too great. Gradually, our eyes became accustomed to the darkness. We stood transfixed, speechless at the treasure we had discovered."

6 A Thief in the Night

Ibn Kayid waited for the sound of snoring from Shamar's hut. When he heard it, he stood up and silently headed for the old woman's hut.

He peered inside, every nerve in his body alert for the sound of someone approaching. There was nothing, apart from the old woman's snores.

His eyes spied the mound of skins and blankets that he knew hid the box that held a forest of fig trees. He silently stepped over Shamar's sleeping body. He felt among the skins and his hand closed around a long wooden box.

The minute he had heard about these figs that grew from twigs, he knew he must have them. If these were planted near the cave in the hills, within a few years he would have a plentiful supply of food to see him through the harsh winters. He clutched the box greedily. Now they were his.

Just as quietly as he had entered the hut, he backed out of it. He gathered his leather pouch, still half full of pistachio nuts, from where he had rested beside the fire. He hid the box beneath the shells and headed to the gates of Gilgal.

With a final glance over his shoulder, Ibn Kayid, the son of the cunning one, was on his way. He hurried towards the hills that lay to the north-east.

By the time the sun rose, a single spire of smoke rose lazily from the charred branches of the village fire.

Fahd kicked the ashes. The stranger was nowhere to be seen. It was unusual for someone to leave without at least bidding his hosts farewell.

Suddenly Fahd wheeled around. A long wail was coming from the direction of his aunt's hut.

"Shamar!" he called. "What is wrong?"

The other villagers, woken by the noise, peered warily out of their stone huts. Fahd ran as fast as his crooked leg would allow him towards his aunt's hut. There, he found the old woman looking distressed and flinging skins and blankets in a pile to one side of the hut.

"It's gone," she wailed. "Next year's forest of figs is gone."

"It was that man who called himself Ghayyath," came a voice behind him. He turned to see his sister, Durriyyah, looking angrily inside the hut. "He calls himself the one who helps? More likely, the one who helps himself."

"We don't know it was him," said Fahd.

"Who else would it be?" hissed Durriyyah.

Shamar nodded her head woefully. "I've been tricked," she said.

"We all have," said Fahd, hurrying across the stones to his hut. He disappeared inside and reappeared seconds later with his heavy stone axe in hand.

"When the other men return, tell them I have headed to the north-east," he said, taking his sister by the shoulders. Then, with a steely gaze, he hitched his skins and his knotted woollen blanket about his shoulders and limped through the gates of Gilgal, in pursuit of the thief.

"As soon as our eyes became accustomed to the gloom inside the cave, we picked our way through the debris that littered the floor. I'd made sure to bring my camera, so we would have photographs of the cave as it was before we disturbed anything.

Everywhere we looked, there were the remnants of human habitation. Stone chips and flakes, some stone tools, strange markings scratched into the walls.

We moved deeper into the cave, photographing it from every angle. Minute by minute, we made our way further and further. Then I froze.

The beam of my torch fell upon a tangle of scattered curves that lay inside a stone circle.

'Is that ...?' said one of my assistants breathlessly.

'Yes,' I said, barely able to contain my excitement. 'It is. It's a skeleton. A human skeleton.'

This site, deep beneath the grove of the *fustuq halabee*, was delivering more than I had ever expected. A Neolithic habitation. And the remains of a human inhabitant."

7 An Ancient Crime

Fahd's progress, unlike the swift animal whose name he carried, was slow. But, despite the pace forced upon him by his injury, he was determined.

He headed north-east and, from time to time, caught tantalising glimpses of his quarry, far in the distance. Disappearing down ravines, or sometimes obscured for hours in the stands of oak or cinnabar trees that dotted the landscape, Ibn Kayid was unaware of his pursuer. But in his haste, he left signs and clues – a broken branch, a footprint, kicked up stones – that Fahd could follow. And, for one day and one night, he did.

Eventually, the thief reached his mountain hideout. He squeezed into the opening in the stone wall his father had built and, for the first time in many weeks, breathed in the cool air of the cave.

Barely an hour passed before an angry call startled him.

"Ghayyath, fig thief, come out and return what you have stolen!"

Ibn Kayid jumped to his feet, his face twisting into a mixture of shock and anger. He recognised the voice.

"Do not enter, for death awaits the wounded cheetah that disturbs my refuge," he threatened.

"Give us back our figs!" demanded Fahd.

Ibn Kayid watched in fury as the entrance to his cave darkened and the figure of Fahd, carrying his fearsome stone axe, squeezed through the entrance. He knew he could not fight the muscular man, even with his damaged leg. His mind whirled. He needed to escape.

Ibn Kayid reached into his pouch and drew out the box of fig cuttings. "One step closer, and I'll destroy them all," he growled. "Go away!"

Fahd, enraged by the stranger's deception, rushed forward. Ibn Kayid emptied the box of twigs and angrily snapped them in half, throwing them at the advancing Fahd. Then he turned to flee, heading for the rear of the cave, knowing there was a smoke vent there that led to the grove of pistachios above him.

Fahd chased the thief but, in the darkness, Ibn Kayid eluded him. Fahd came upon a stone fireplace and looked up. There, the thief was scrambling up the rocks. With his damaged leg, Fahd knew he would never be able to climb the rocks. Instead, he whirled and raced back to the entrance of the cave in a rage. He started to climb the hillside, heading for where he guessed the smoke vent would be found. With grim satisfaction, he saw a head and shoulders emerge from behind a rock. With a speed that belied his injury, Fahd raced up to the rock. He swung his axe and there was a sickening thump. Ibn Kayid's body went limp. He slowly slid back down the vent.

"After about thirty minutes in the cave, we headed back to the entrance. On the way, I noticed something we had missed in our excitement. About twenty metres in, there was a small wooden box and, scattered around, there were ancient, broken twigs.

In order to avoid their being disturbed on any future exploration of the cave, I picked them up.

When we came to the exit, my spirits fell. I could see that the bright sunshine had disappeared, replaced by ominous dark clouds rolling in from the east. I shouldn't have been surprised. The heavy rainfalls that marked the end of autumn were long overdue.

Ten minutes later, as we huddled inside one of the tents up on the plateau, recounting our first sight of the cave and its contents, heavy raindrops began to fall. Then came the downpour. Bitterly disappointed, we all knew that the exploration of the site would have to wait until the rains had passed. That afternoon, wet and bedraggled, we fixed tarpaulins over the entrance to the cave and resigned ourselves to spending another three months waiting.

But those three months proved critical in putting together the story of our cave and its occupant. If you recall, at the start of this speech, I mentioned the work of my colleagues in 2006, on the west bank of the Jordan River.

There, at the site of a dig named Gilgal 1, a far-reaching discovery was made. Among the stone huts of an ancient Neolithic village, archaeologists had found the remains of figs. The fruits were mutant figs – growing on a rare kind of tree that wasn't pollinated by insects and wouldn't reproduce unless someone took a cutting and planted it. This, ladies and gentlemen, was the first evidence of a remarkable change in human civilisation.

The knowledge of how to grow plants from cuttings marked the transition from a hunter-gatherer society to an agricultural one. The act of planting trees, and understanding how to encourage young saplings to grow, was one of the most important steps we humans have ever undertaken.

A few days after the rains had closed our site, it occurred to me that I should send the twigs I had recovered from the cave to one of the people I knew had worked at Gilgal 1.

One month later, I received an astonishing reply. These twigs were from exactly the same kind of fig – but the cave was located almost sixty kilometres away from Gilgal 1. How could that be?

The next day, I hired a car and drove straight to the Jordan Archaeological Museum in Amman. I needed to check the exhibits, to see if there were any other similarities I might find between the artefacts of Gilgal 1 and the cave.

For the rest of the week, I made detailed notes about all the stone artefacts recovered from the dig on the west bank of the river. But it was not until I was able to return to the cave that I made the most fascinating discovery of all.

Last month, ladies and gentlemen, the weather in Jordan had settled down enough for a return to the grove of the *fustuq halabee*. My first task was to examine the skeleton I had found lying near the ancient stone fireplace. And when I did, I was startled.

Within the first few seconds, it became clear that this was no poor human who had been trapped in the cave or who had died of natural causes. One look at the skull, crushed violently, was enough to confirm one thing.

This was a murder.

And, having spent a week examining the minutest details of the artefacts from Gilgal 1, I had a growing suspicion as to what the murder weapon had been.

On display at the Jordan Archaeological Museum, there had been a mighty stone axe that had been recovered from one of the ruins at Gilgal 1.

I rushed the skull to the museum and, within a couple of hours, they rang to confirm. The dimensions of the wound and of the axe matched.

Suddenly, we had an ancient crime scene. We had an ancient weapon that seemed to fit the bill. We had twigs from a species of fig that had mysteriously turned up sixty kilometres from where they were expected to be."

Melissa Fox looked out across the sea of enthralled faces. She lowered her voice and prepared to wind up her speech.

"We will never know exactly what happened there, ten thousand years ago. But there are too many links between these two sites for us to imagine that there is not some connection. We can only guess at what sinister events link these two places.

But I will leave you with a thought, ladies and gentlemen. For many years, we assumed that civilisation spread through human society by the sharing of knowledge passed down between families and communities. What would it say about us, as a species, if this discovery was to demonstrate exactly the opposite? That civilisation spread through violence and theft."

The audience was silent. It was indeed an awful thought.

"Think of all the ideas and inventions we see today – all protected jealously by corporations and governments, never shared. Are we really so different from our Neolithic ancestors? Or are we the same, merely separated by ten thousand years?"

Melissa Fox looked out over the audience, challenging them to think about how knowledge might really have spread in the forgotten days of human prehistory.

"That, ladies and gentlemen, is a question I shall leave you to ponder."